GRAPHIC MYTHICAL CREATURES

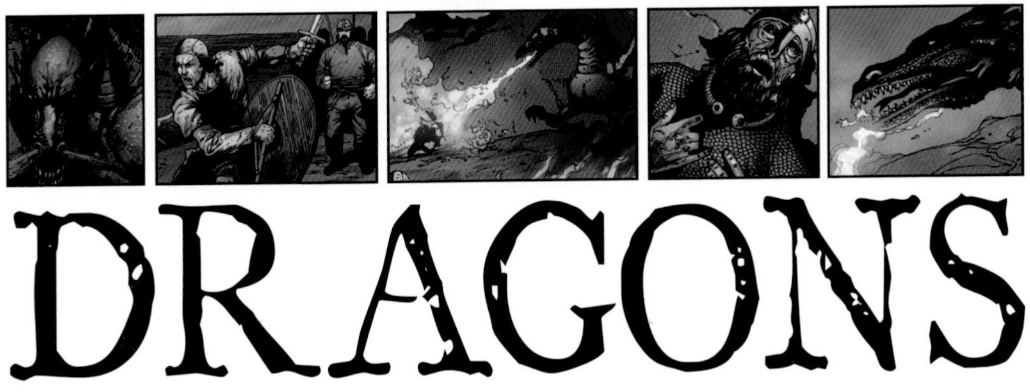

DRAGONS

BY GARY JEFFREY
ILLUSTRATED BY DHEERAJ VERMA

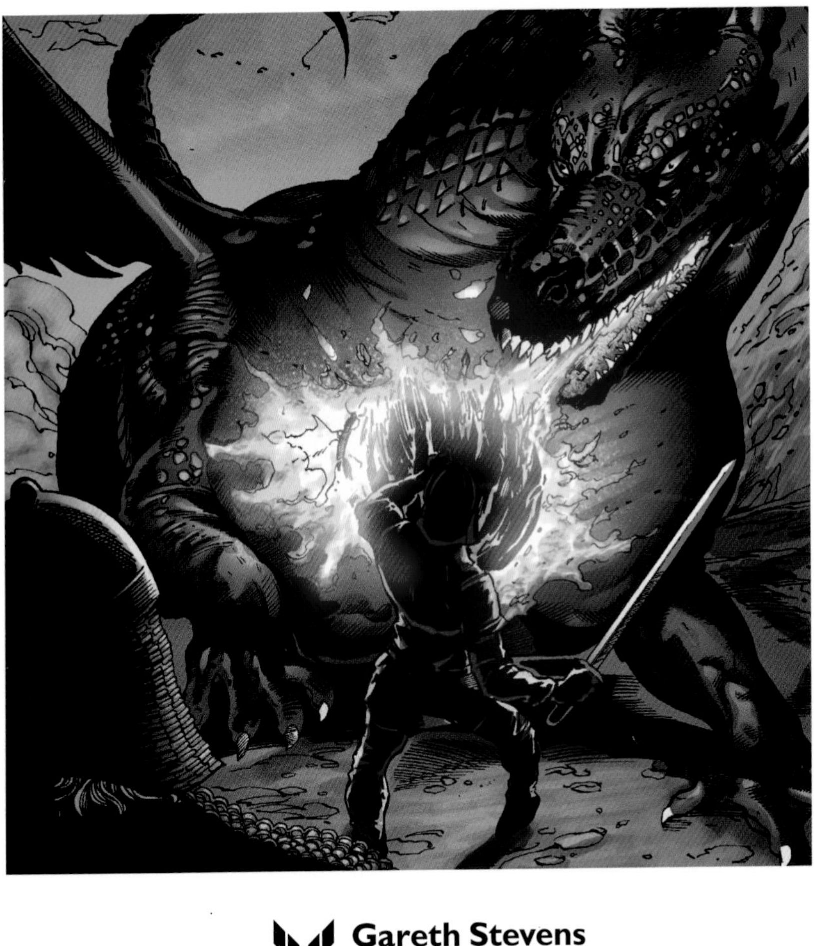

Gareth Stevens
Publishing

Please visit our website, www.garethstevens.com.
For a free color catalog of all our high-quality books,
call toll free 1-800-542-2595 or fax 1-877-542-2596.

Library of Congress Cataloging-in-Publication Data

Jeffrey, Gary.
Dragons / Gary Jeffrey.
p. cm. — (Graphic mythical creatures)
Includes index.
ISBN 978-1-4339-6032-1 (pbk.)
ISBN 978-1-4339-6033-8 (6-pack)
ISBN 978-1-4339-6031-4 (library binding)
1. Dragons—Juvenile literature.. I. Title.
GR830.D7J44 2011
398.24'54—dc22
                                    2010048671

First Edition

Published in 2012 by
Gareth Stevens Publishing
111 East 14th Street, Suite 349
New York, NY 10003

Designed by David West Books
Editor: Ronne Randall

Printed in China

CPSIA compliance information: Batch #DS11GS: For further information contact Gareth Stevens, New York, New York at 1-800-542-2595.

CONTENTS

The World of Dragons

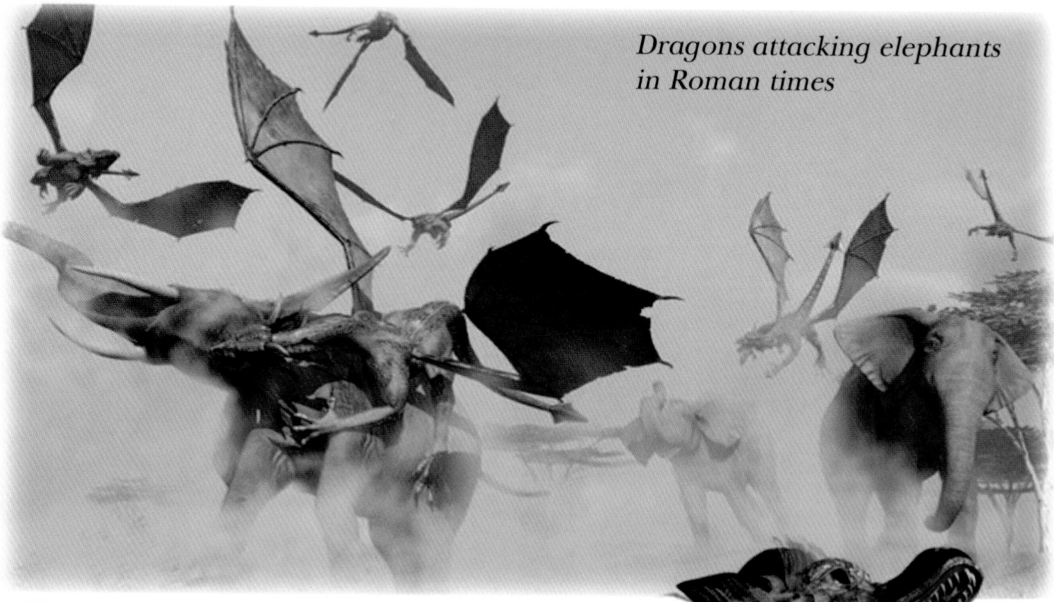

Dragons attacking elephants in Roman times

Dragons have been around since ancient times. The ancient Roman naturalist Pliny wrote that *"dragons crave elephant blood in the summer"* and that *"Ethiopian dragons migrate to Arabia once a year to find food."*

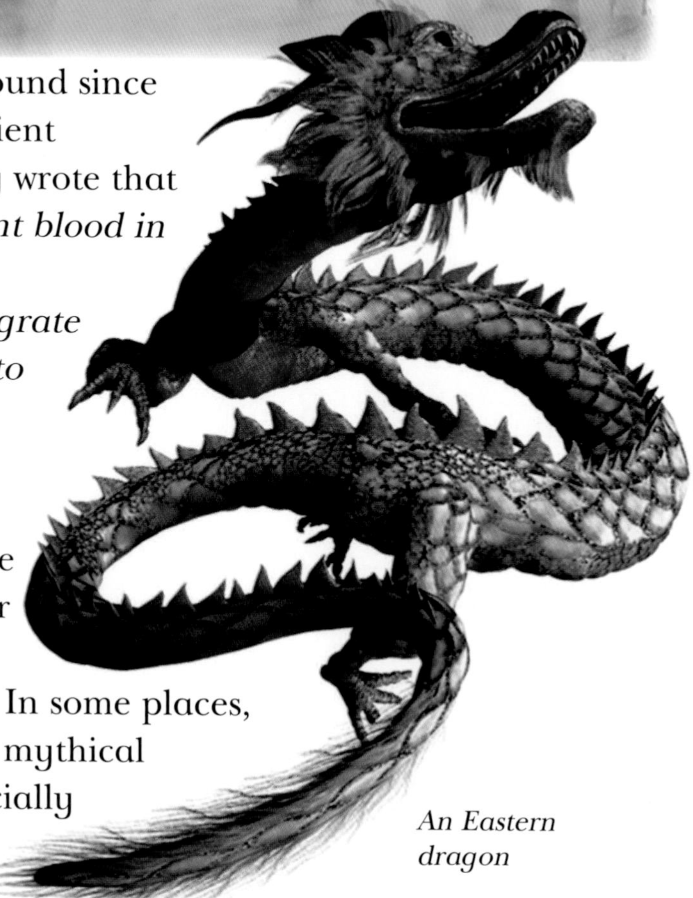

An Eastern dragon

Eastern Dragons

In the East, dragons are symbols of good luck or health and are sometimes worshipped. In some places, they are believed to be mythical rulers of weather, especially rain and water. They don't have wings, but use magic to make them fly.

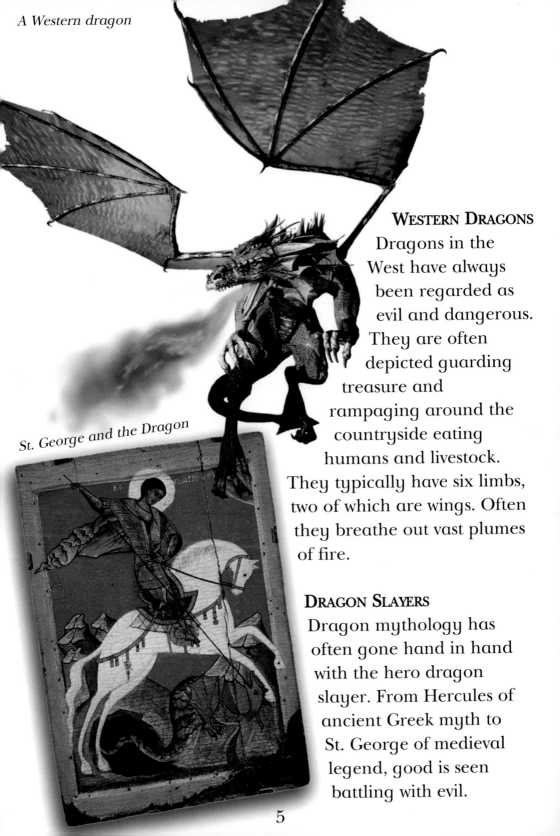

A Western dragon

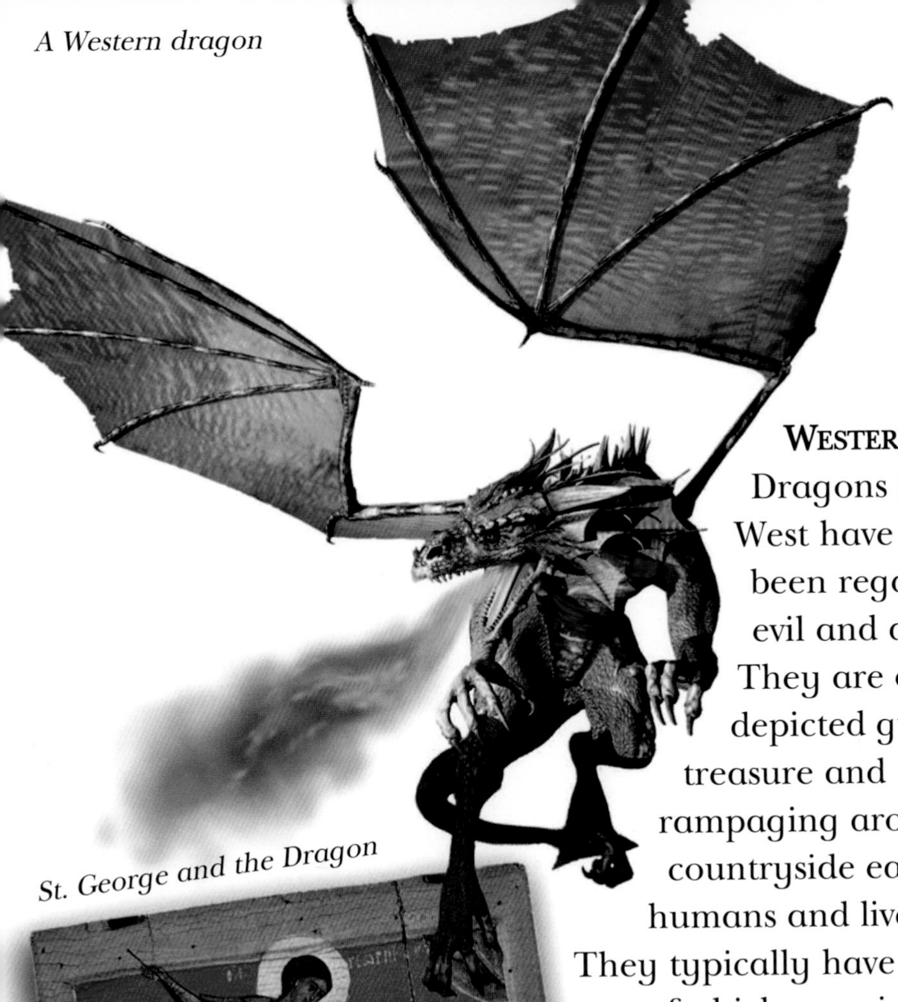

Western Dragons

Dragons in the West have always been regarded as evil and dangerous. They are often depicted guarding treasure and rampaging around the countryside eating humans and livestock. They typically have six limbs, two of which are wings. Often they breathe out vast plumes of fire.

St. George and the Dragon

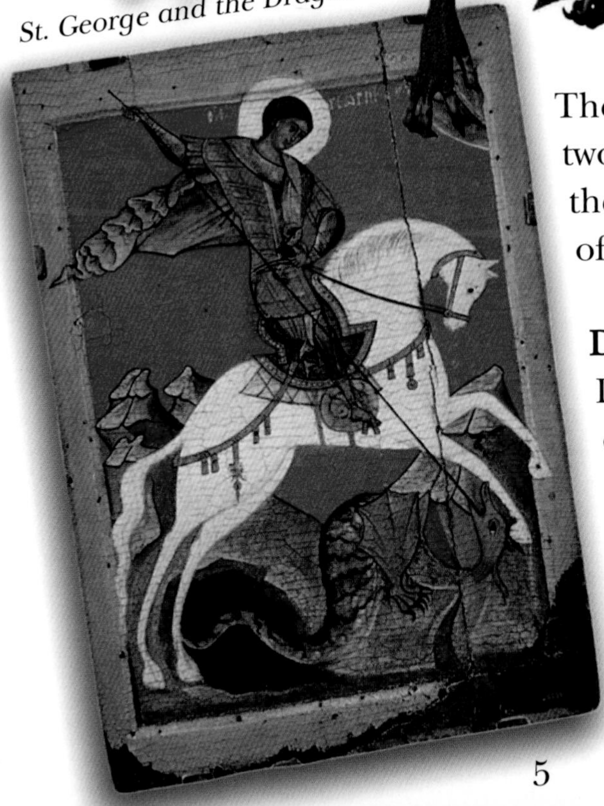

Dragon Slayers

Dragon mythology has often gone hand in hand with the hero dragon slayer. From Hercules of ancient Greek myth to St. George of medieval legend, good is seen battling with evil.

Beowulf and the Dragon

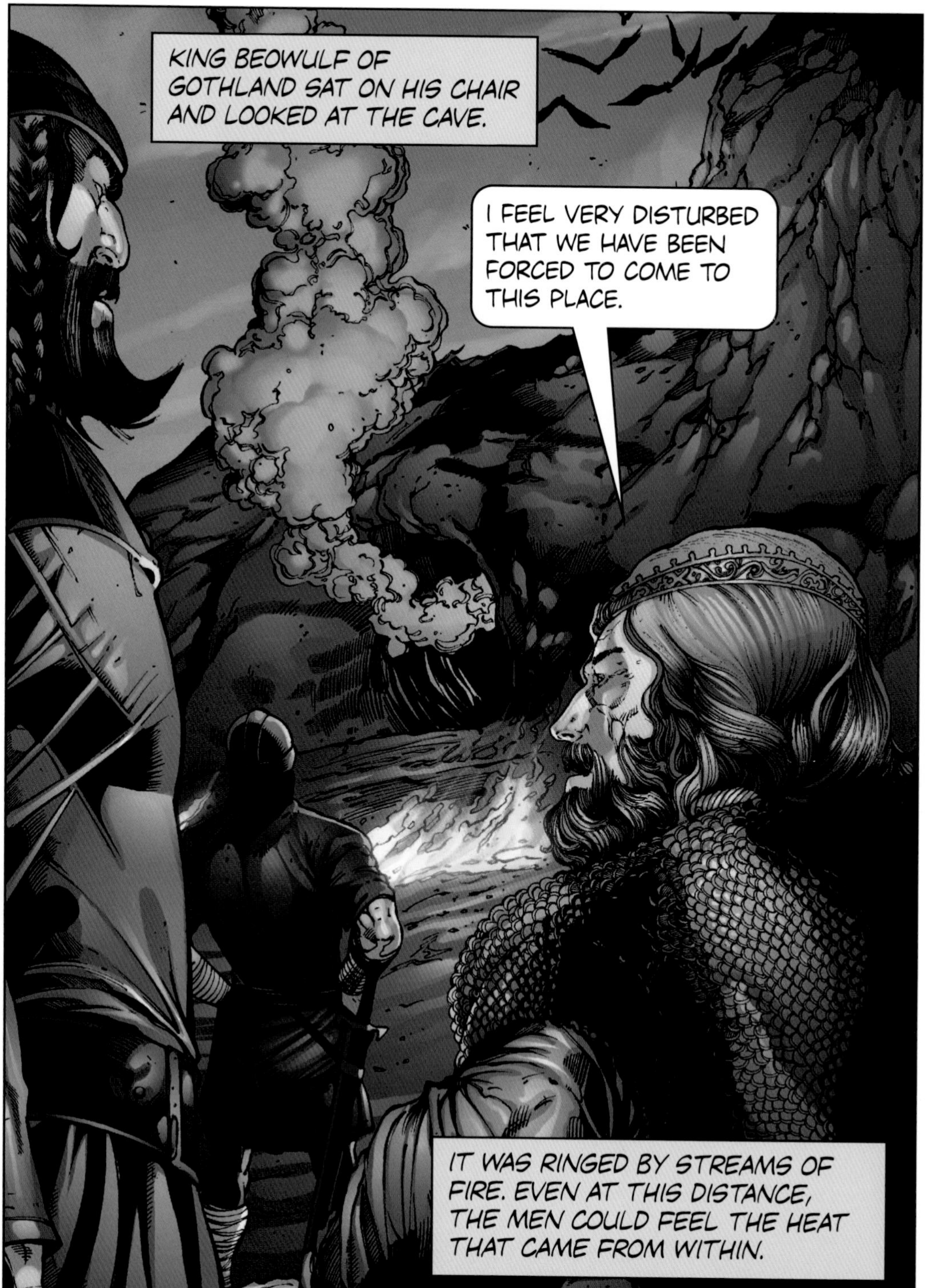
KING BEOWULF OF GOTHLAND SAT ON HIS CHAIR AND LOOKED AT THE CAVE.
I FEEL VERY DISTURBED THAT WE HAVE BEEN FORCED TO COME TO THIS PLACE.
IT WAS RINGED BY STREAMS OF FIRE. EVEN AT THIS DISTANCE, THE MEN COULD FEEL THE HEAT THAT CAME FROM WITHIN.

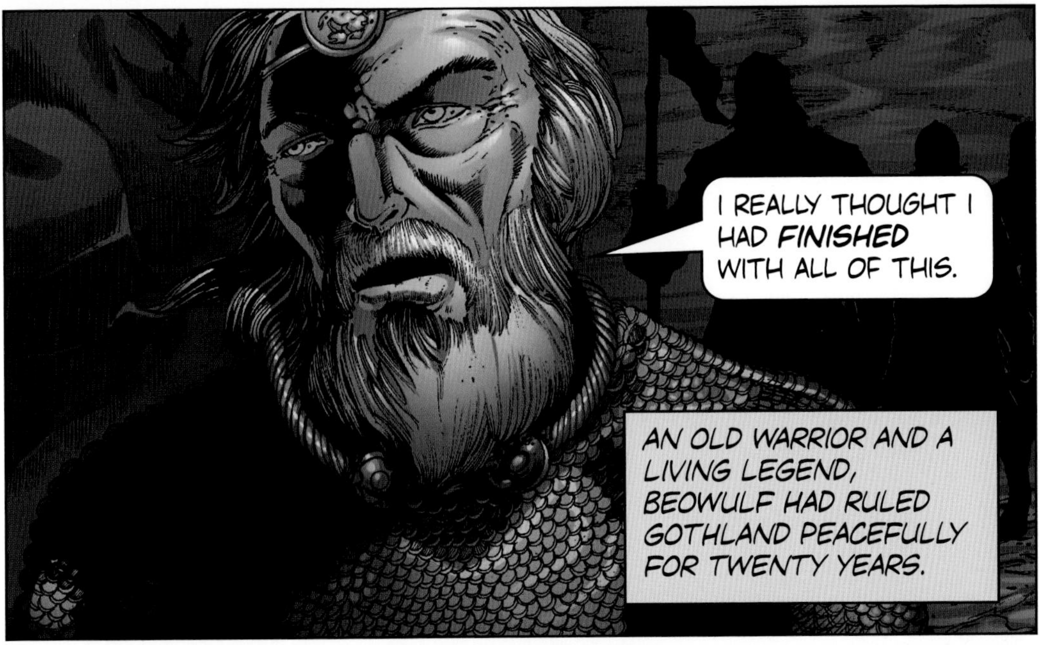
I REALLY THOUGHT I HAD FINISHED WITH ALL OF THIS.
AN OLD WARRIOR AND A LIVING LEGEND, BEOWULF HAD RULED GOTHLAND PEACEFULLY FOR TWENTY YEARS.

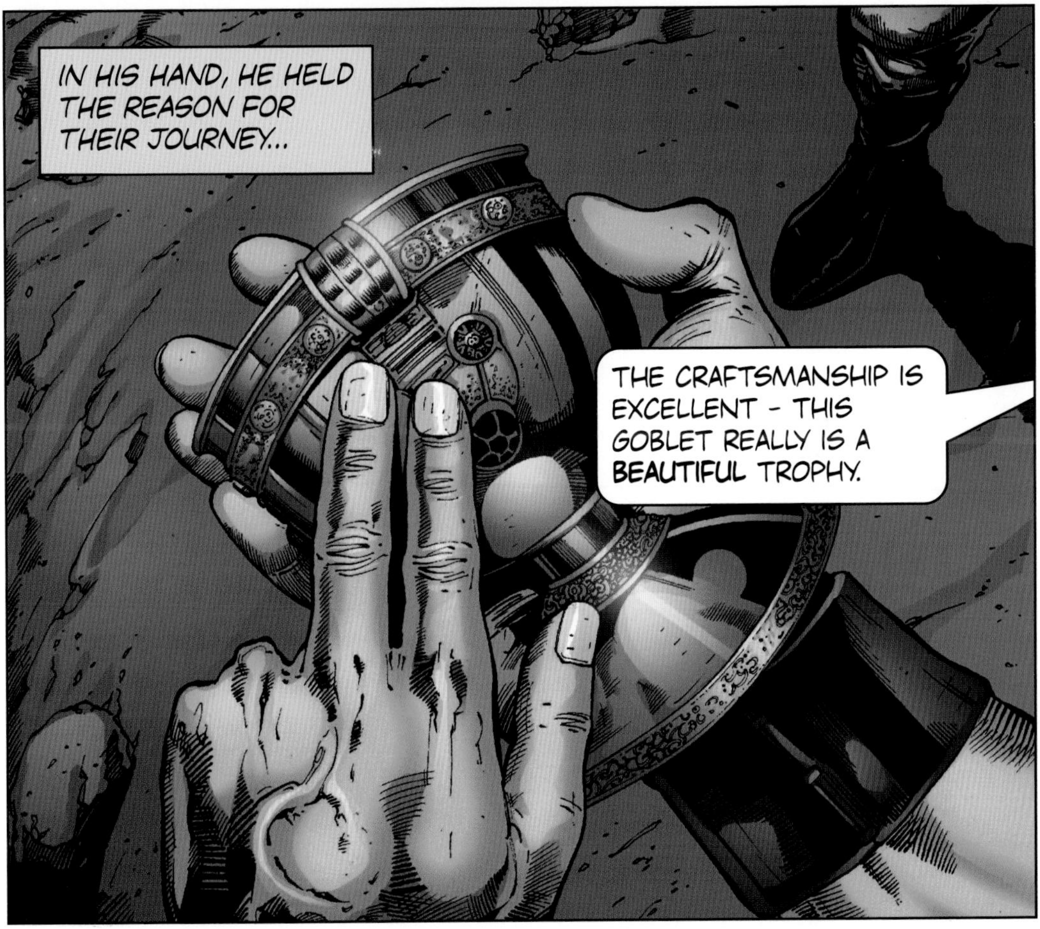
IN HIS HAND, HE HELD THE REASON FOR THEIR JOURNEY...
THE CRAFTSMANSHIP IS EXCELLENT - THIS GOBLET REALLY IS A BEAUTIFUL TROPHY.

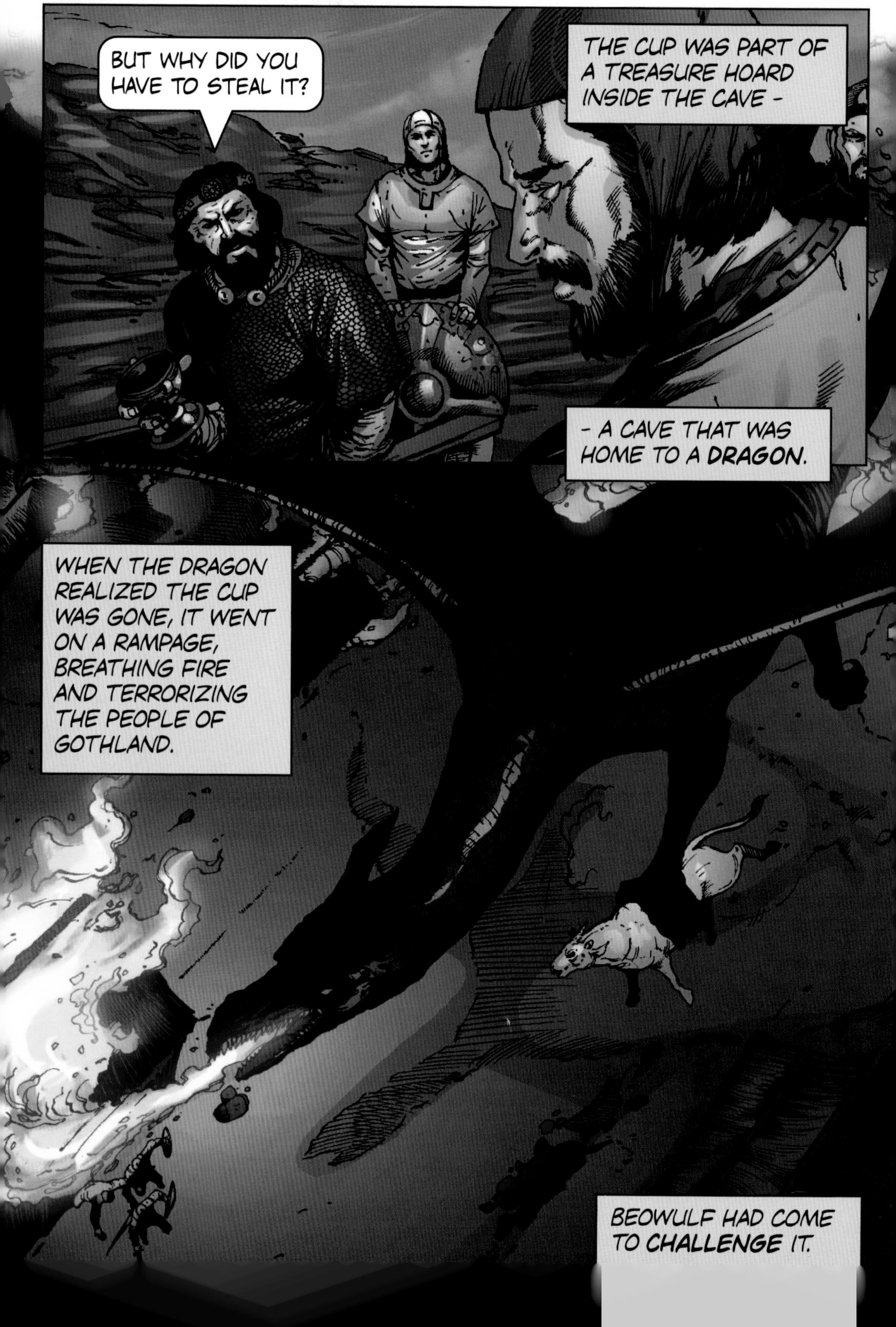
BUT WHY DID YOU HAVE TO STEAL IT?
THE CUP WAS PART OF A TREASURE HOARD INSIDE THE CAVE -
- A CAVE THAT WAS HOME TO A DRAGON.
WHEN THE DRAGON REALIZED THE CUP WAS GONE, IT WENT ON A RAMPAGE, BREATHING FIRE AND TERRORIZING THE PEOPLE OF GOTHLAND.
BEOWULF HAD COME TO CHALLENGE IT.

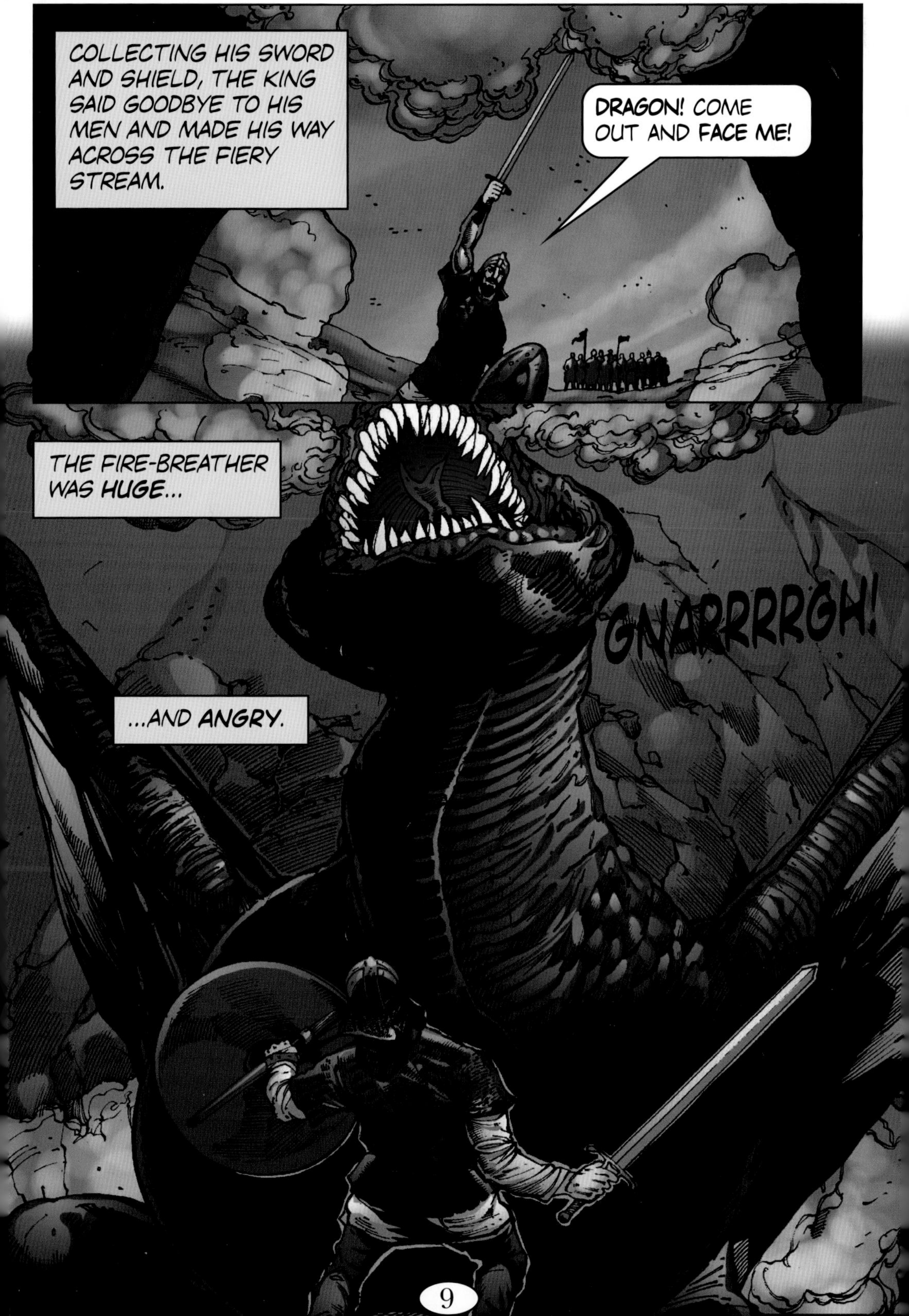
COLLECTING HIS SWORD AND SHIELD, THE KING SAID GOODBYE TO HIS MEN AND MADE HIS WAY ACROSS THE FIERY STREAM.
DRAGON! COME OUT AND FACE ME!
THE FIRE-BREATHER WAS HUGE...
GNARRRRGH!
...AND ANGRY.

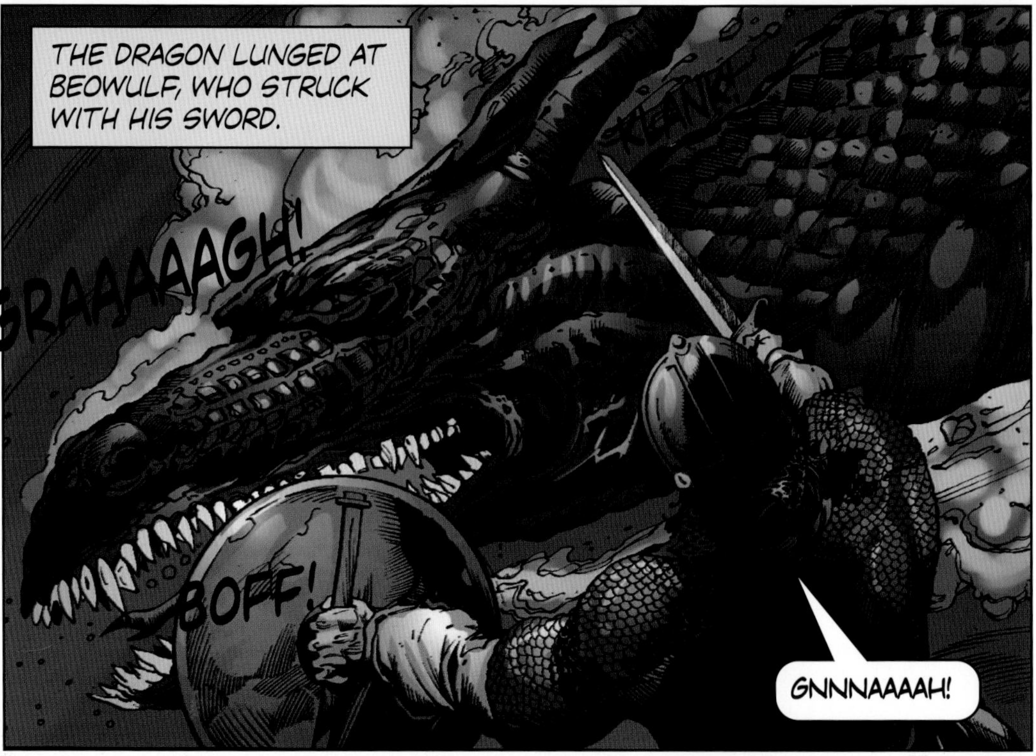
THE DRAGON LUNGED AT BEOWULF, WHO STRUCK WITH HIS SWORD.
GRAAAAAGH!
BOFF!
GNNNAAAAH!

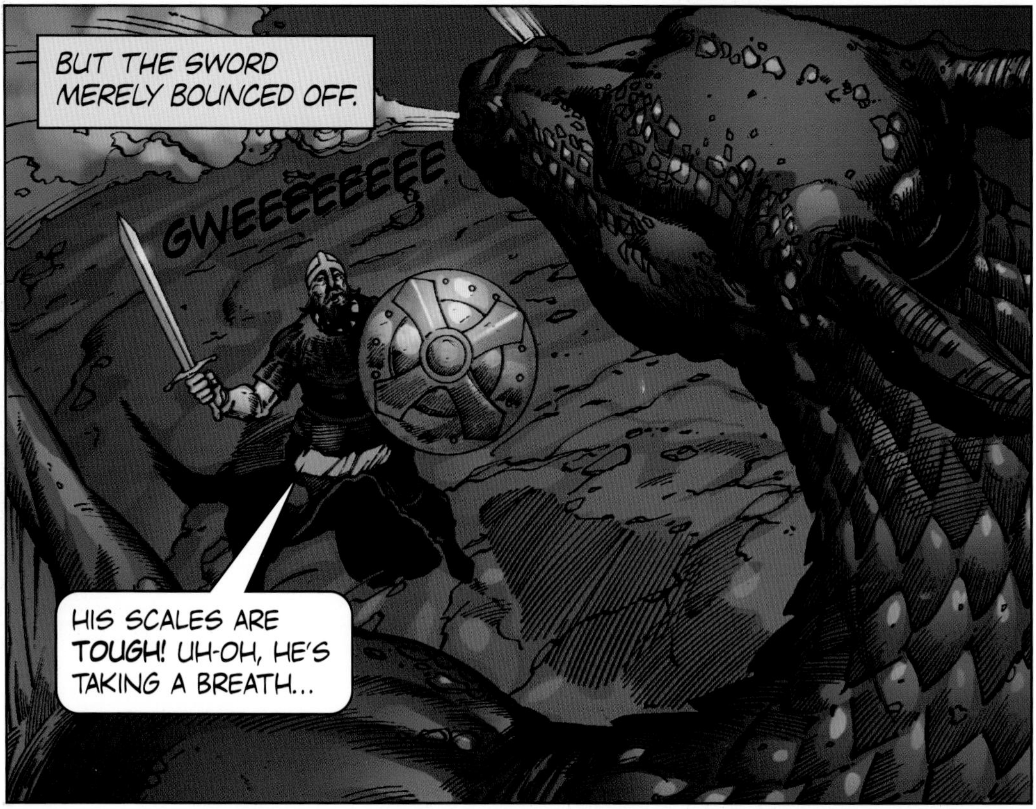
BUT THE SWORD MERELY BOUNCED OFF.
GWEEEEEEEEE
HIS SCALES ARE **TOUGH!** UH-OH, HE'S TAKING A BREATH...

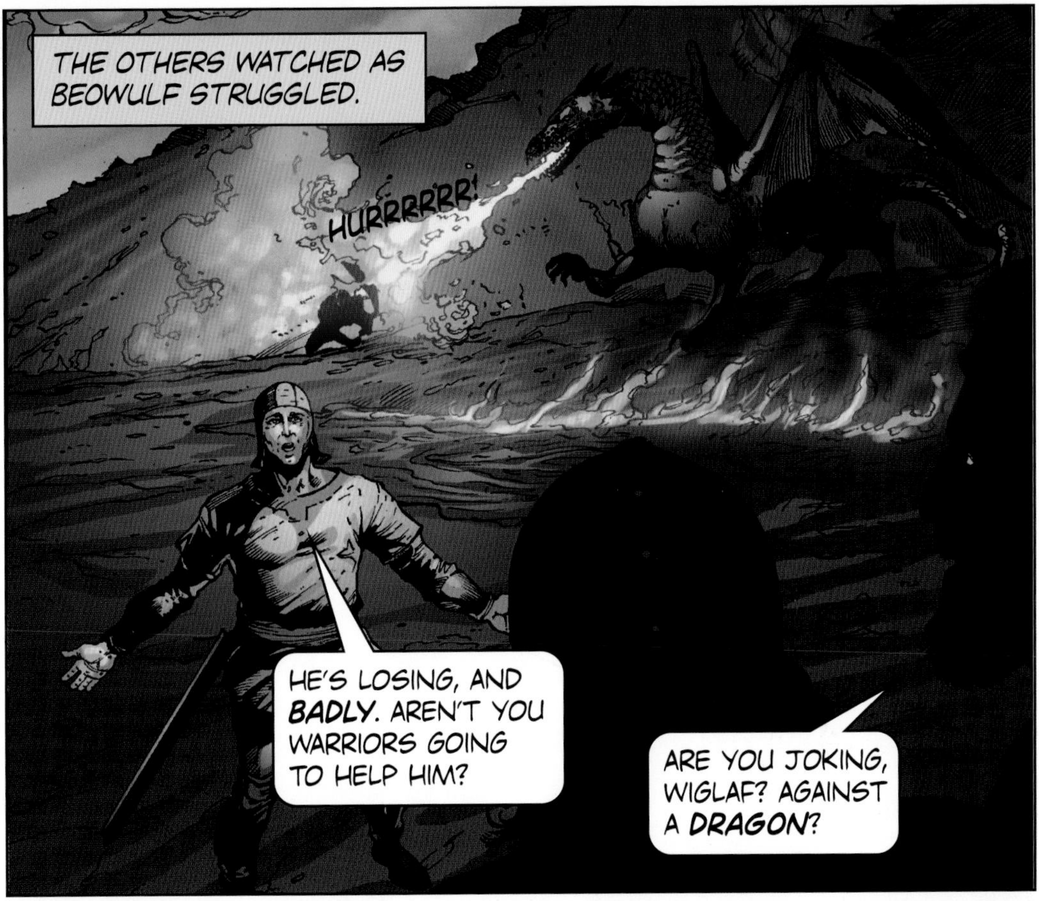
THE OTHERS WATCHED AS BEOWULF STRUGGLED.
HURRRRRR!
HE'S LOSING, AND BADLY. AREN'T YOU WARRIORS GOING TO HELP HIM?
ARE YOU JOKING, WIGLAF? AGAINST A DRAGON?

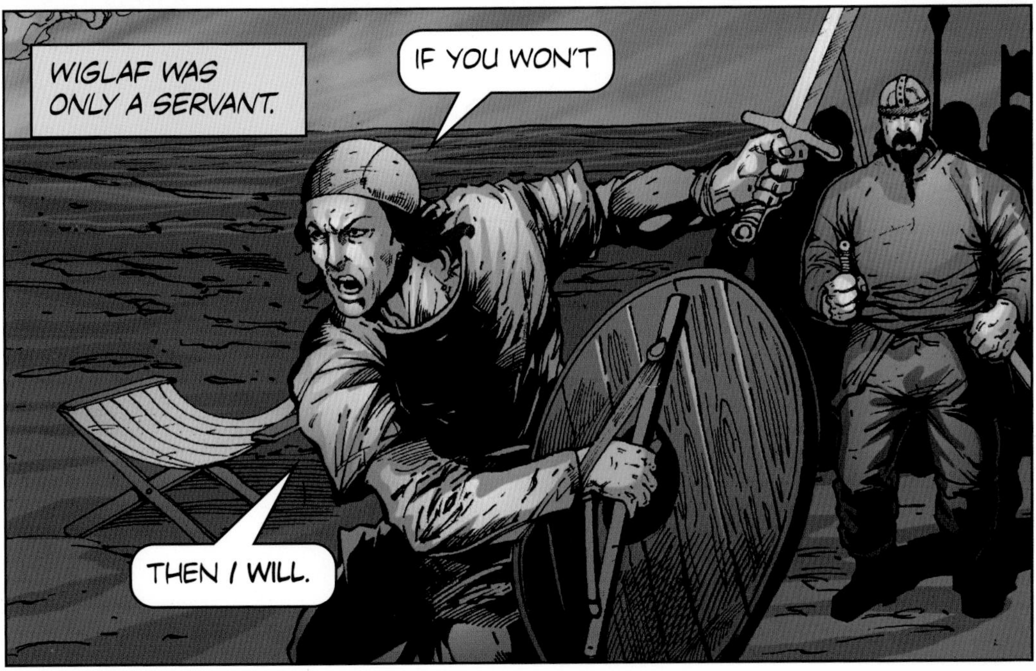
WIGLAF WAS ONLY A SERVANT.
IF YOU WON'T
THEN I WILL.

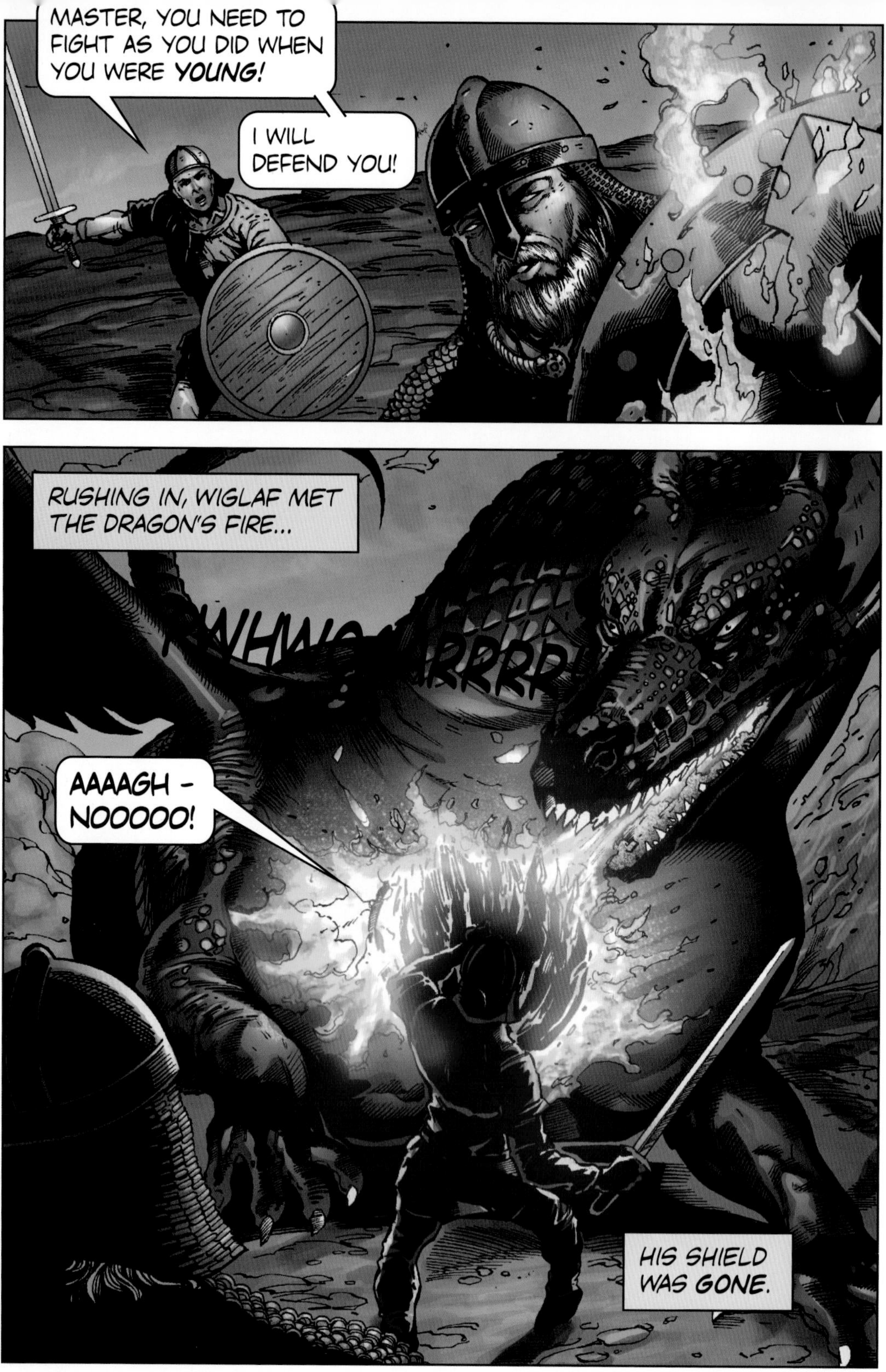
MASTER, YOU NEED TO FIGHT AS YOU DID WHEN YOU WERE YOUNG!
I WILL DEFEND YOU!
RUSHING IN, WIGLAF MET THE DRAGON'S FIRE...
AAAAGH - NOOOOO!
HIS SHIELD WAS GONE.

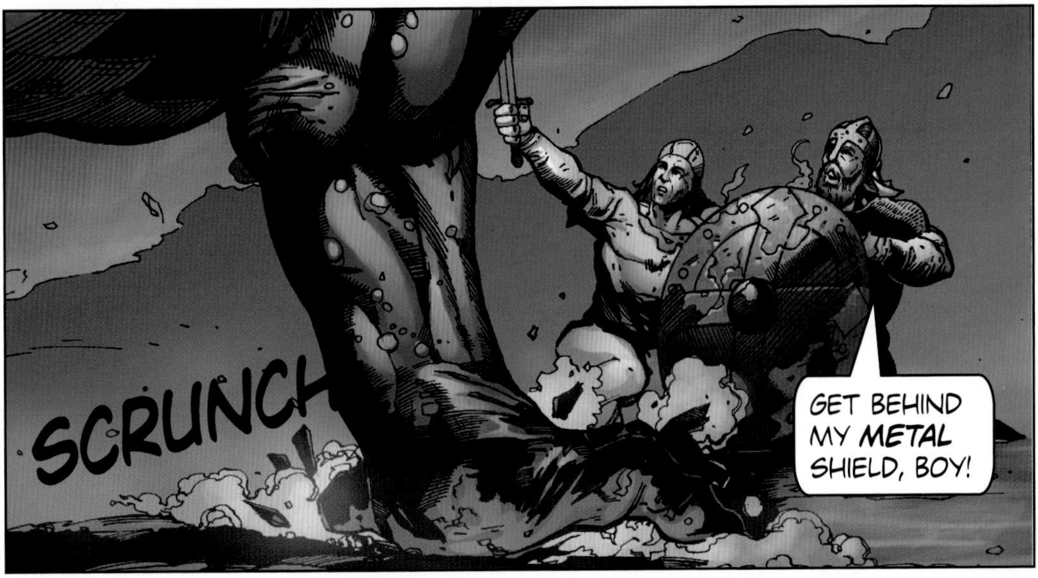
SCRUNCH
GET BEHIND MY **METAL** SHIELD, BOY!

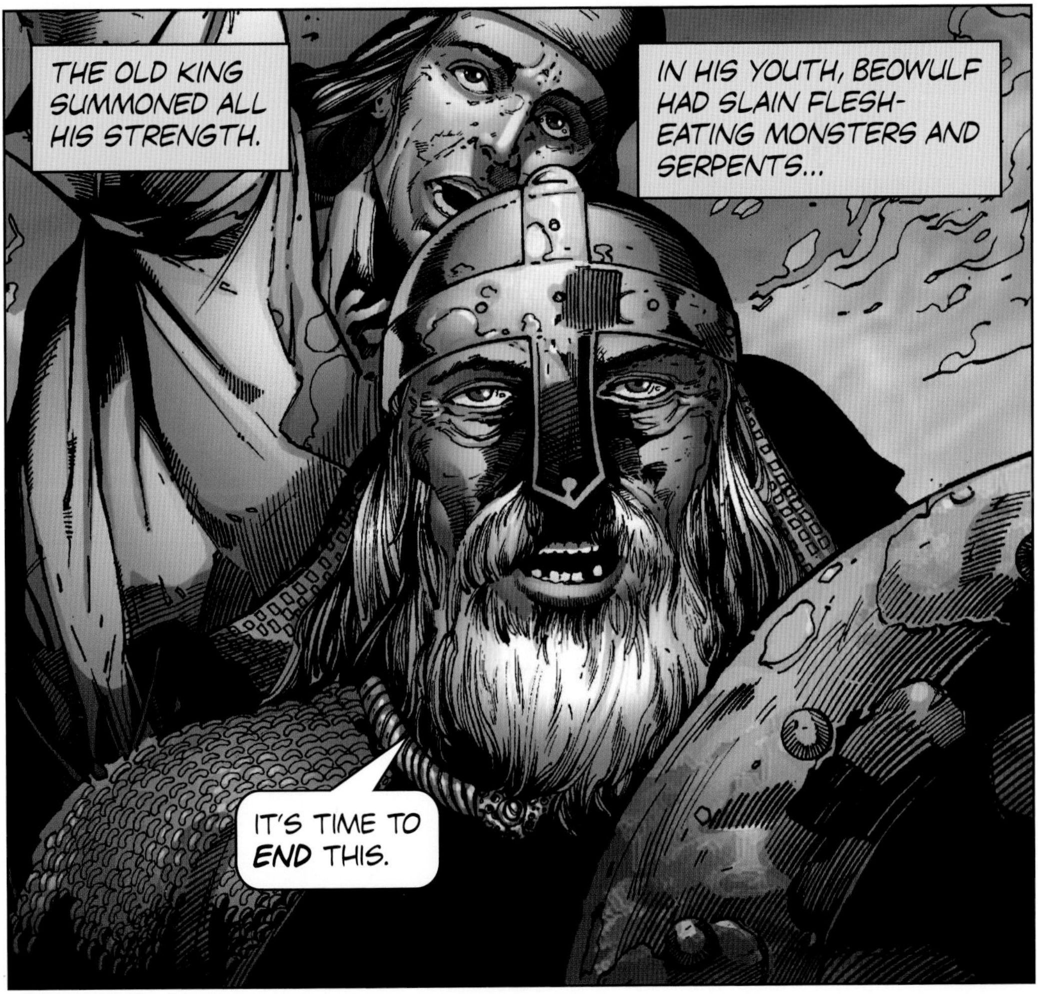
THE OLD KING SUMMONED ALL HIS STRENGTH.
IN HIS YOUTH, BEOWULF HAD SLAIN FLESH-EATING MONSTERS AND SERPENTS...
IT'S TIME TO **END** THIS.

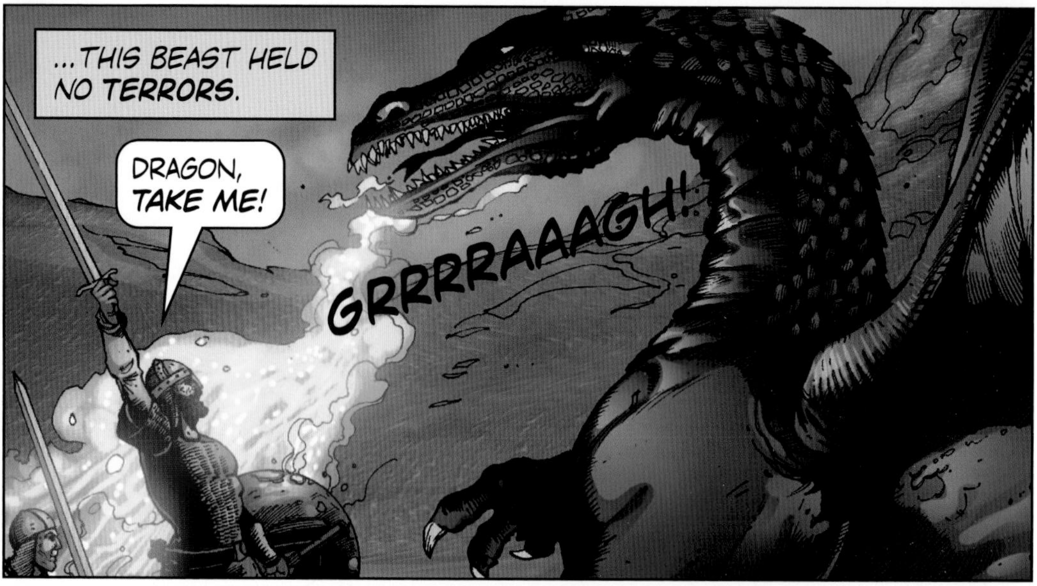
...THIS BEAST HELD NO TERRORS.
DRAGON, TAKE ME!
GRRRRAAAGH!

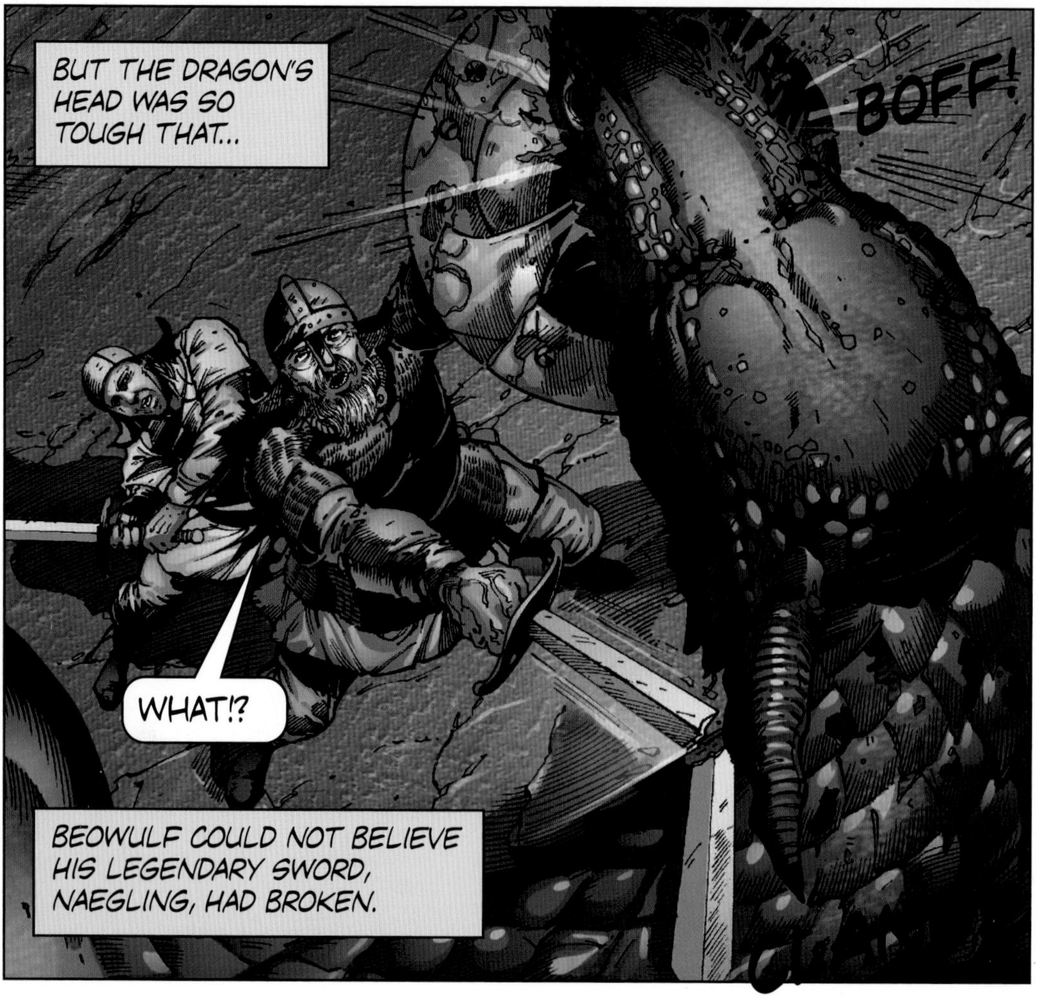
BUT THE DRAGON'S HEAD WAS SO TOUGH THAT...
BOFF!
WHAT!?
BEOWULF COULD NOT BELIEVE HIS LEGENDARY SWORD, NAEGLING, HAD BROKEN.

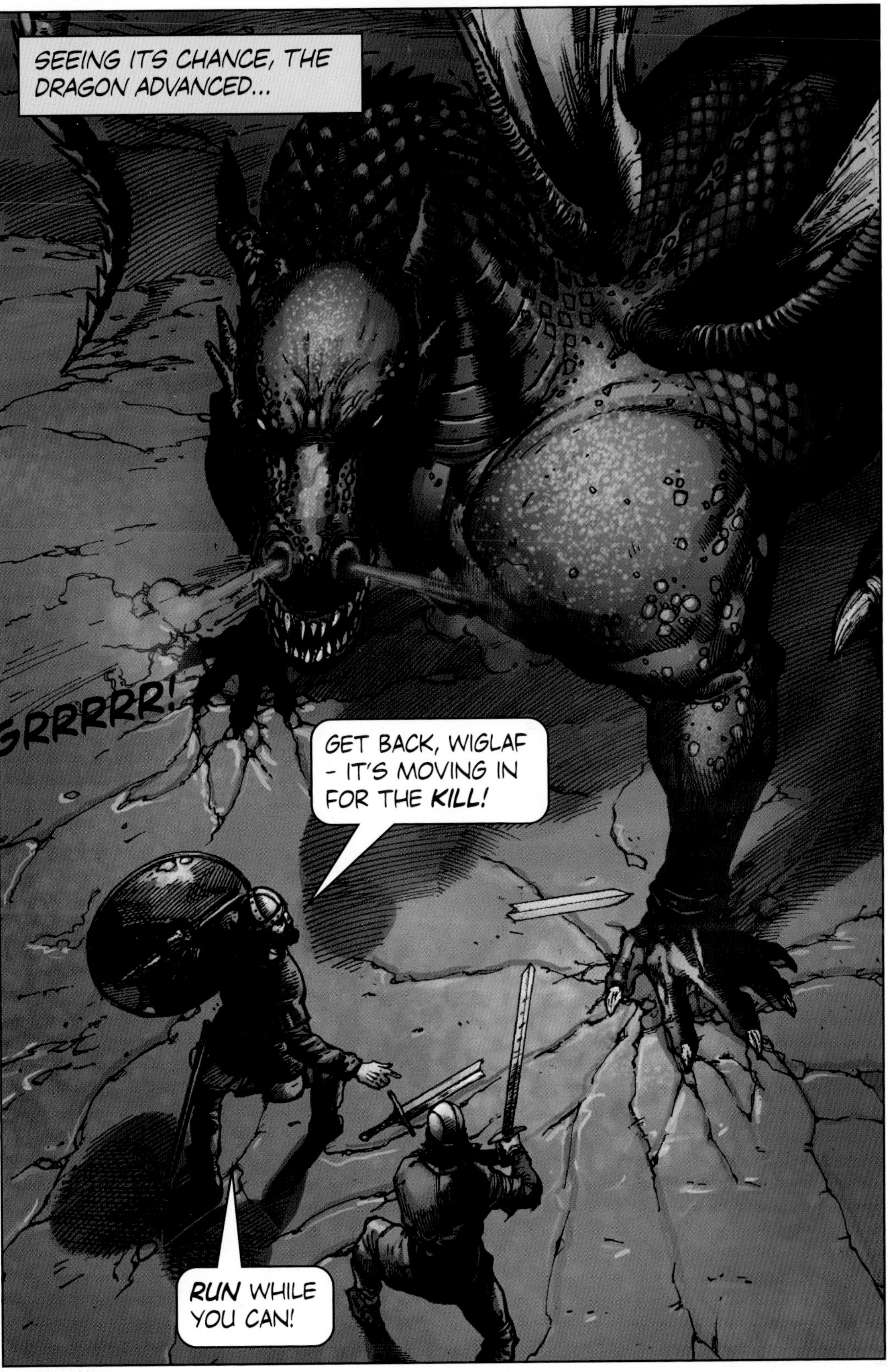
SEEING ITS CHANCE, THE DRAGON ADVANCED...
GRRRRR!
GET BACK, WIGLAF - IT'S MOVING IN FOR THE KILL!
RUN WHILE YOU CAN!

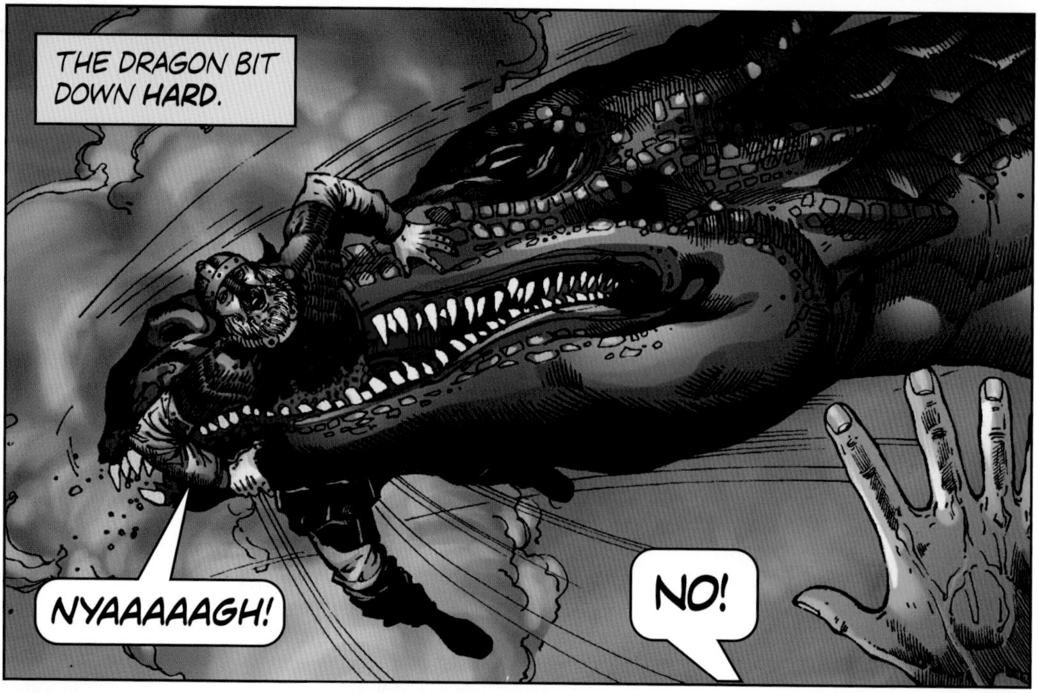
THE DRAGON BIT DOWN HARD.
NYAAAAAGH!
NO!

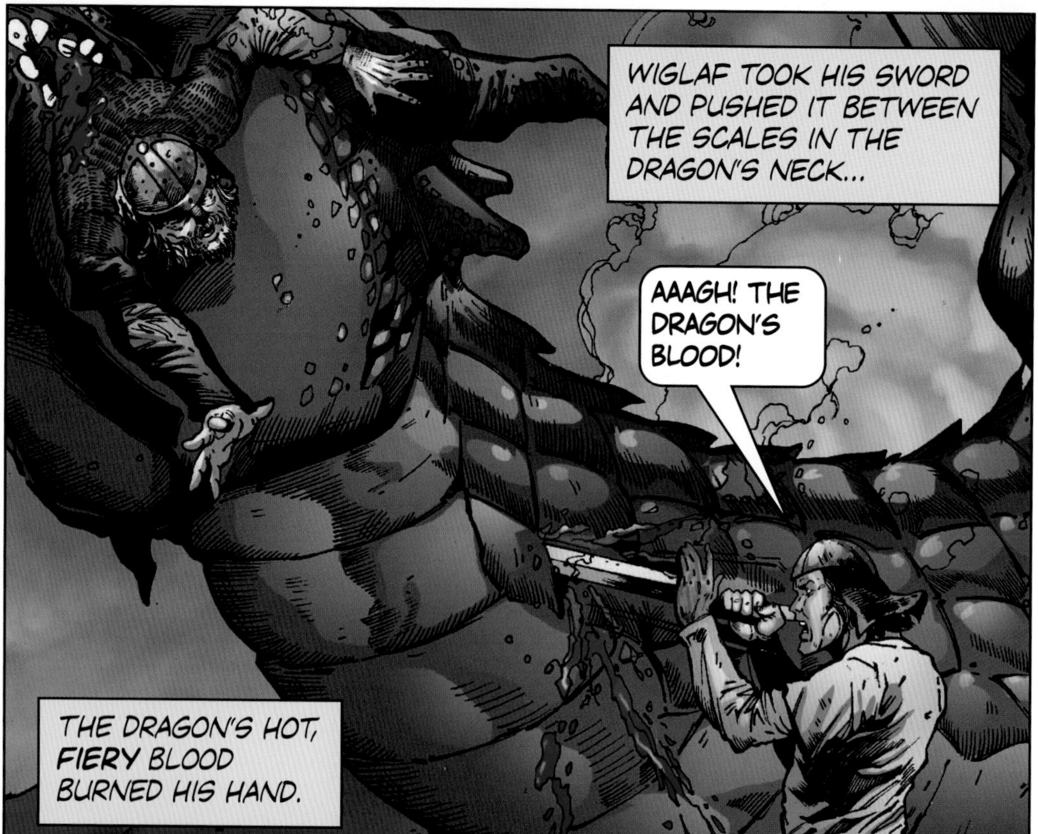
WIGLAF TOOK HIS SWORD AND PUSHED IT BETWEEN THE SCALES IN THE DRAGON'S NECK...
AAAGH! THE DRAGON'S BLOOD!
THE DRAGON'S HOT, FIERY BLOOD BURNED HIS HAND.

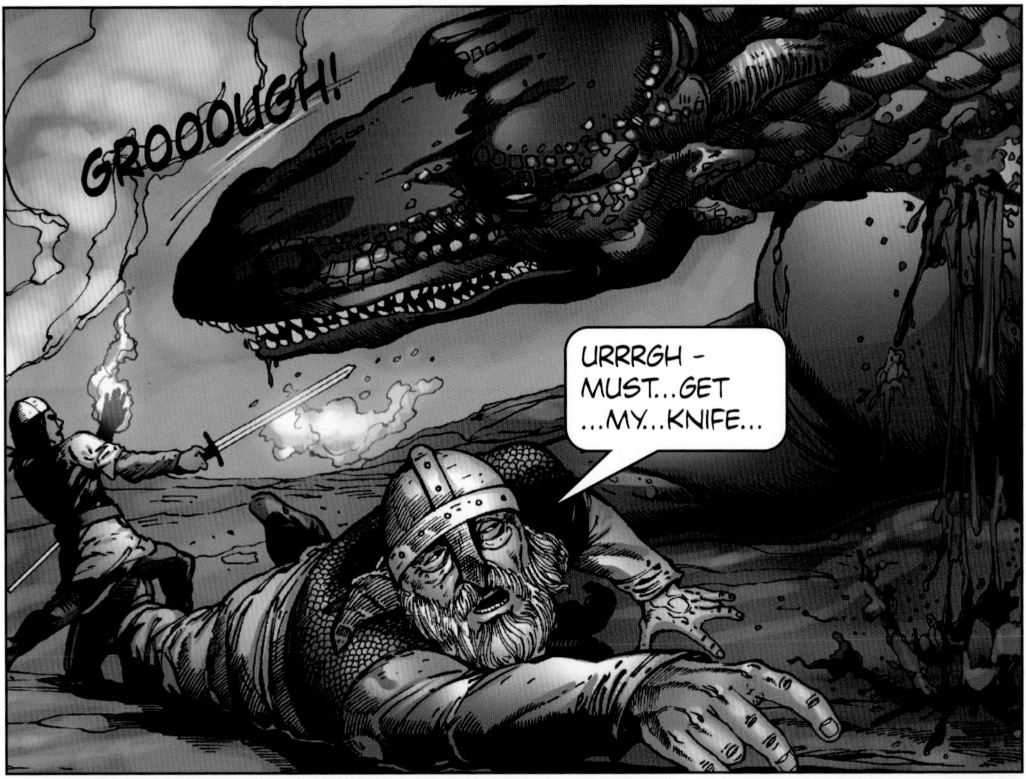
GROOOUGH!
URRRGH - MUST...GET ...MY...KNIFE...

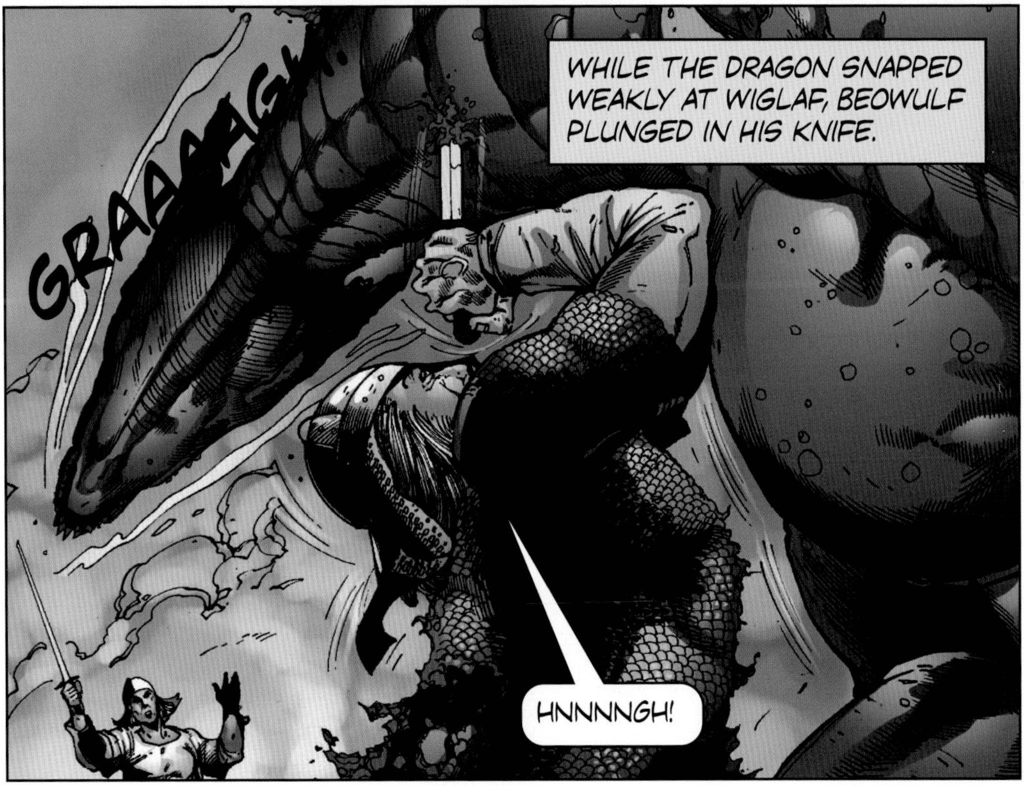
WHILE THE DRAGON SNAPPED WEAKLY AT WIGLAF, BEOWULF PLUNGED IN HIS KNIFE.
GRAAAAGH!
HNNNNGH!

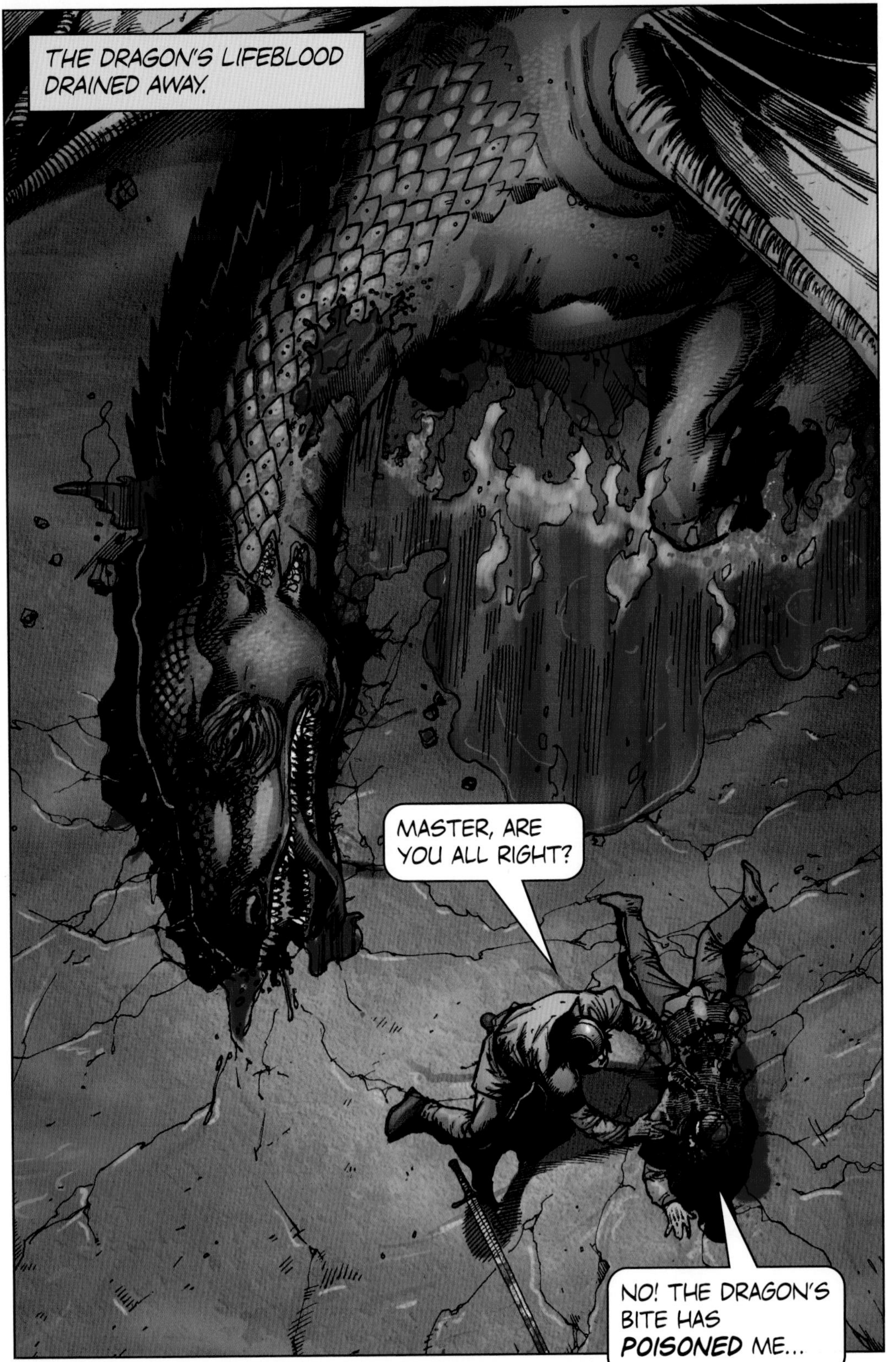
THE DRAGON'S LIFEBLOOD DRAINED AWAY.
MASTER, ARE YOU ALL RIGHT?
NO! THE DRAGON'S BITE HAS **POISONED** ME...

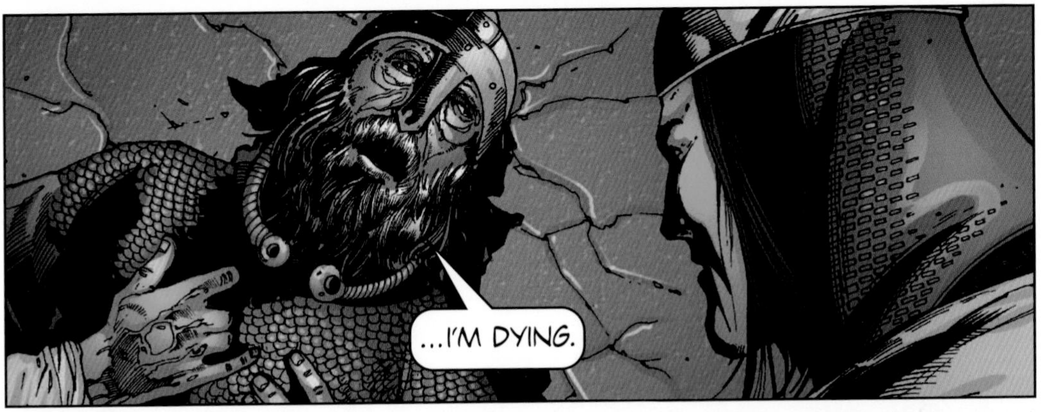
...I'M DYING.

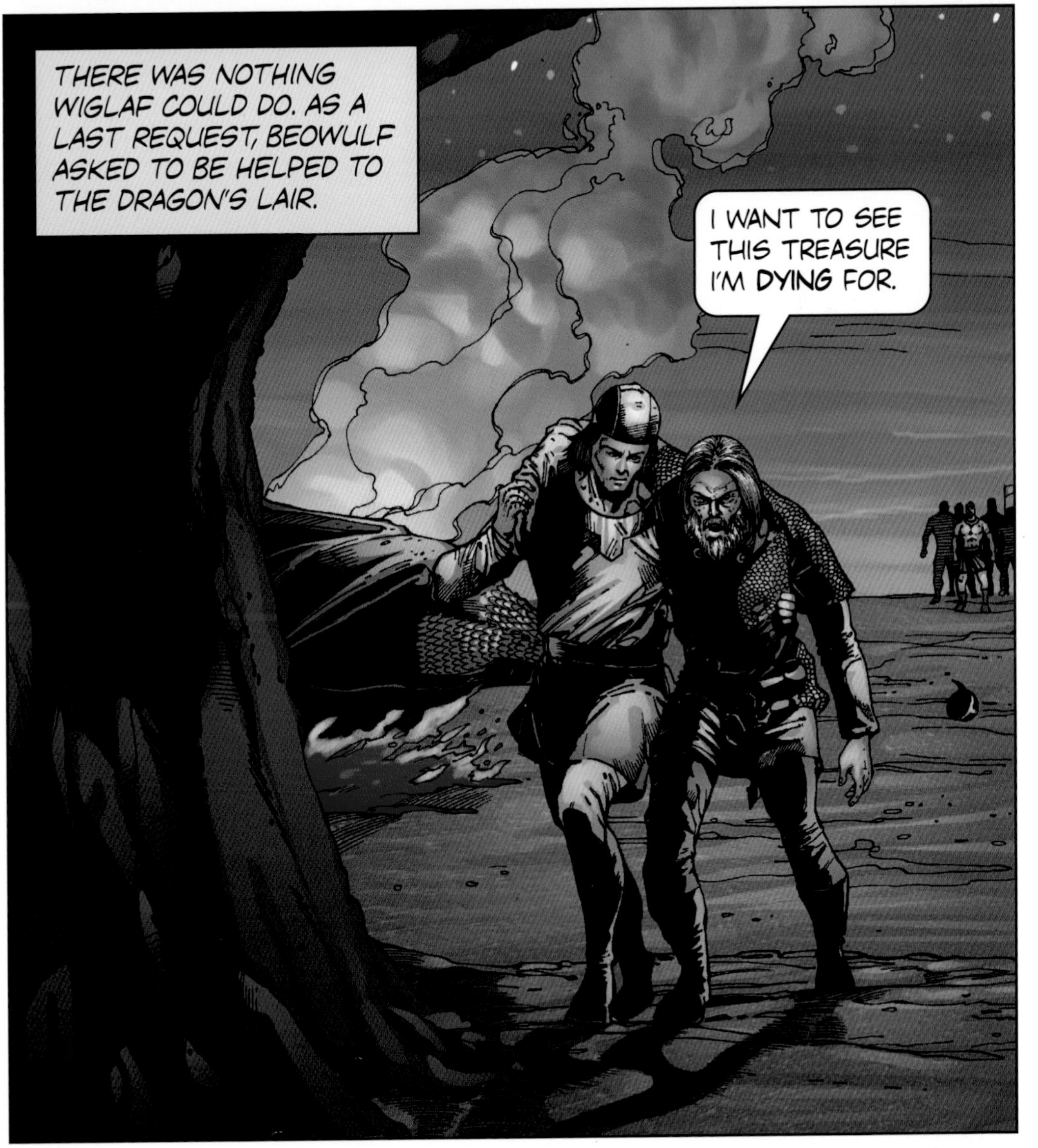
THERE WAS NOTHING WIGLAF COULD DO. AS A LAST REQUEST, BEOWULF ASKED TO BE HELPED TO THE DRAGON'S LAIR.
I WANT TO SEE THIS TREASURE I'M **DYING** FOR.

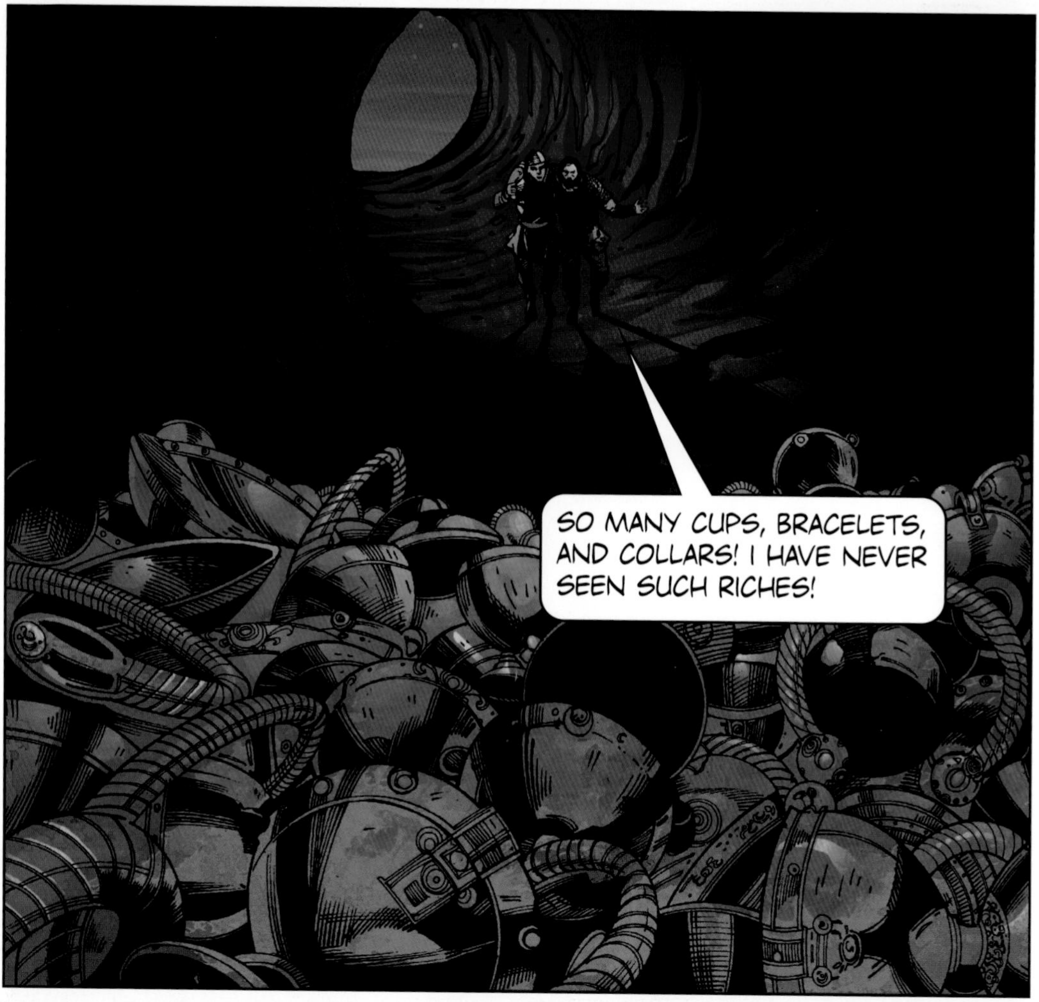
SO MANY CUPS, BRACELETS, AND COLLARS! I HAVE NEVER SEEN SUCH RICHES!

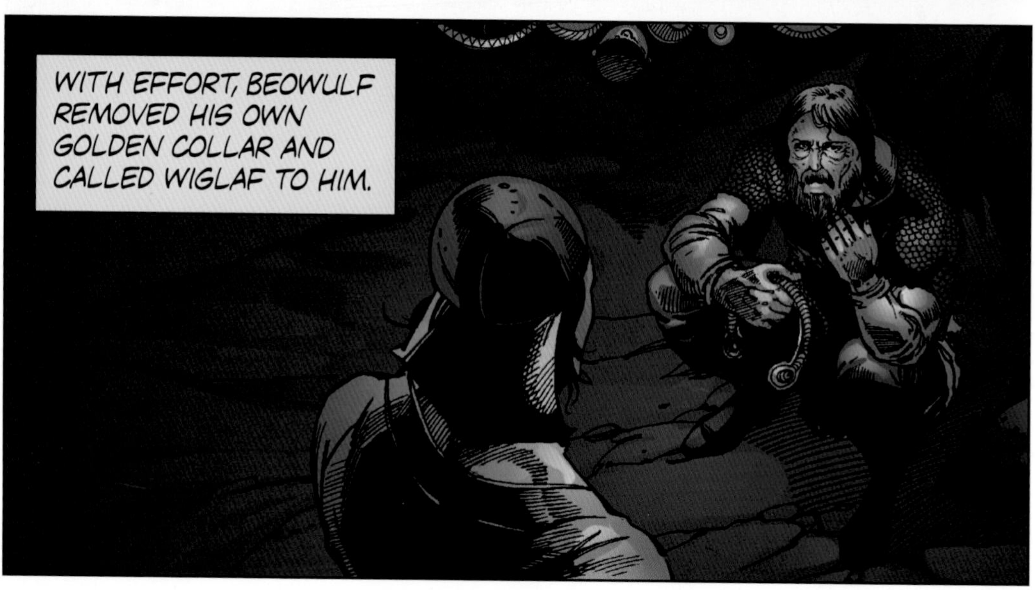
WITH EFFORT, BEOWULF REMOVED HIS OWN GOLDEN COLLAR AND CALLED WIGLAF TO HIM.

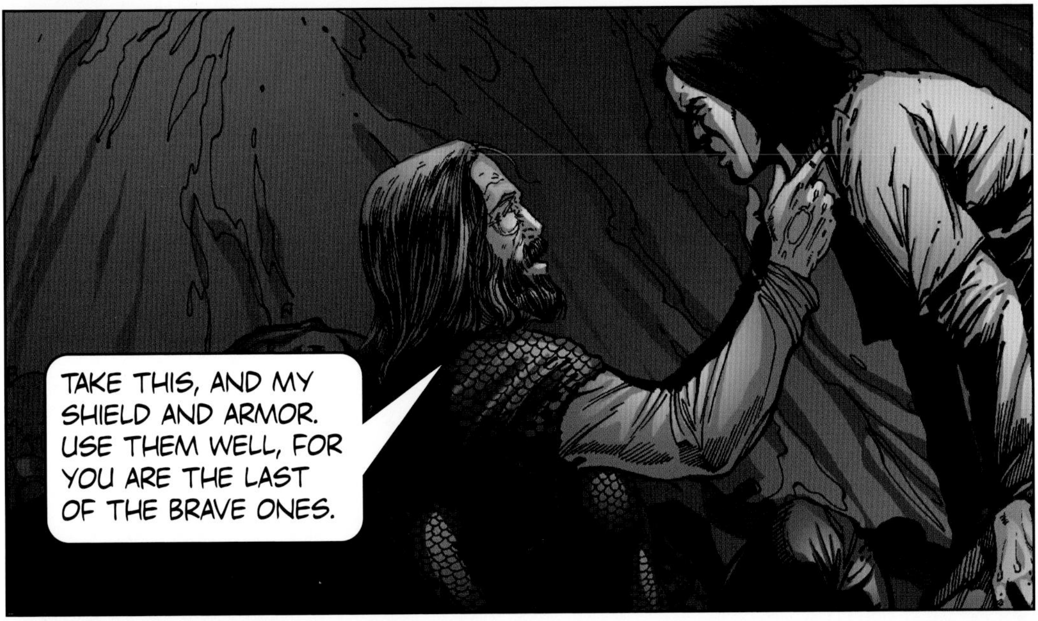
TAKE THIS, AND MY SHIELD AND ARMOR. USE THEM WELL, FOR YOU ARE THE LAST OF THE BRAVE ONES.

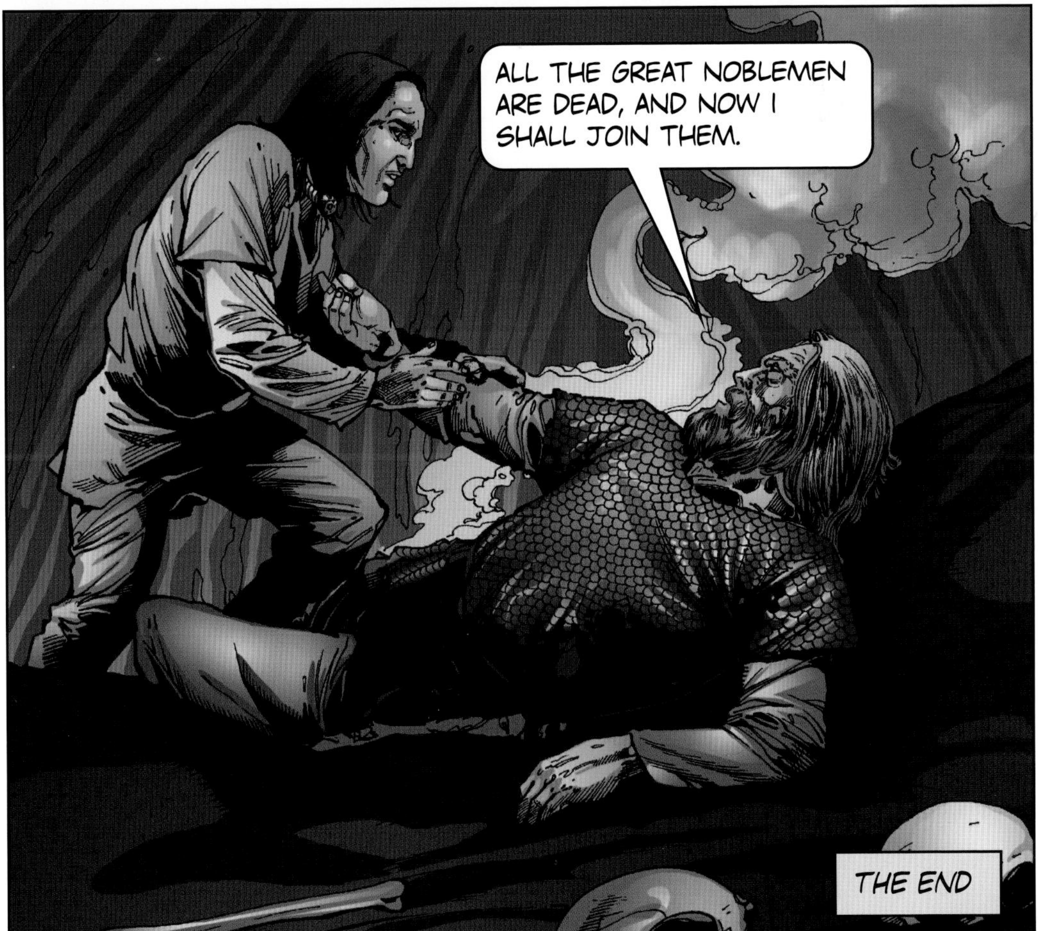
ALL THE GREAT NOBLEMEN ARE DEAD, AND NOW I SHALL JOIN THEM.
THE END

Other Famous Dragons

The source for Beowulf and the dragon is an old Anglo-Saxon poem, but dragons feature in myths and legends from all over the world. Here are some of the more well-known dragon tales.

St. George and the Dragon
The story of how the traveling English saint rescues a princess who had been offered to a dragon as a sacrifice.

Maud and the Wyvern
This medieval story tells of a young girl who finds a baby wyvern (a four-limbed dragon) and keeps it as a secret pet, with terrible results.

Kiyohime and the Tale of Dojoji
A story from Japanese folklore in which a waitress, Kiyohime, learns how to turn herself into a flying dragon to punish a man who rejected her.

Rostam and Rakhsh
An ancient Persian hero named Rostam is saved by his horse, Rakhsh, when an invisible dragon creeps up on him while he is sleeping.

Sigurd and Fafnir
An ancient Norse story involving trickery, dragons' blood, and magical changes.

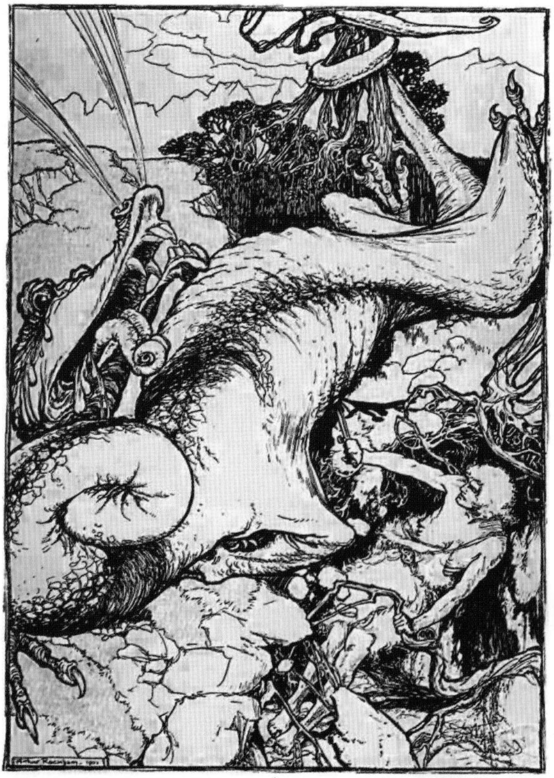

Sigurd kills the dragon Fafnir in its lair.

GLOSSARY

crave To feel a powerful want for something.

hoard A collection of valuable objects that are carefully guarded.

livestock Valuable farm animals.

lunge To make a sudden forward movement to strike at something.

migrate To move regularly from one region to another, depending on the season.

naturalist An expert in natural history.

plumes Long clouds of smoke or fire that look like feathers as they spread out.

rampaging Rushing around being violent and out of control.

serpent A dragon or mythical, snake-like reptile.

summoned Called forth.

terrorizing Putting a horrible feeling of fear into people.

trophy A hard-won prize.

vast Huge and sweeping.

INDEX